Aunts, uncles, cousins—
they are our relatives.

If mommy or daddy has a sister, she is your aunt.

If mommy or daddy has a brother, he is your uncle.

If your aunts or uncles have children,

When you take a plane trip
to visit relatives,

Cousins exchange presents.

You can watch family videos
with cousins.

You can call a cousin on the telephone.

A cousin gives you clothes he has outgrown.

You can be in a wedding with a cousin.

Cousins pose for silly pictures together.

Cousins are for sleep-overs.

You can dance with a cousin.

It's nice to have cousins.
How many cousins do you have?